"In a moment, the chariot races will begin," said Plato. "Winning a chariot race is the greatest honour of the games."

Jack just nodded. He was still studying the short soldier, who seemed to be looking back at him.

Suddenly a small hand came out from the soldier's cape. The hand gave a little wave.

Jack gasped. It was Annie's hand waving!

The short soldier was *Annie*.

Read all the adventures of Jack and Annie!

Magic Tree House™

Olympic Challenge!

MARY POPE OSBORNE

Illustrated by Philippe Masson

RED FOX

To Chase Goddard, who loves to read

OLYMPIC CHALLENGE! 978 1 782 95386 9
A RED FOX BOOK

First published in Great Britain by Red Fox,
an imprint of Random House Children's Publishers UK
A Random House Group Company

Published in the US as *Hour of the Olympics* by Random House Children's Publishers UK
division of Random House Inc, 1998

Red Fox edition published 2010

The Random House Group Limited supports the Forest Stewardship
Council® (FSC®), the leading international forest-certification
organisation. Our books carrying the FSC label are printed on
FSC®-certified paper. FSC is the only forest-certification scheme
supported by the leading environmental organisations, including
Greenpeace. Our paper procurement policy can be found at
www.randomhouse.co.uk/environment

MIX
Paper from
responsible sources
FSC® C016897

Red Fox Books are published by Random House Children's Publishers UK
61–63 Uxbridge Road, London W5 5SA
www.**kids**at**randomhouse**.co.uk

Addresses for companies within The Random House Group Limited
can be found at: www.randomhouse.co.uk/offices.htm

THE RANDOM HOUSE GROUP Limited Reg. No. 954009

A CIP catalogue record for this book is available from the British Library.

Printed and bound by CPI Group (UK) Ltd, Croydon, CR0 4YY

Contents

Dear Readers,

Olympic Challenge! was a joy for me to write, mostly because Jack and Annie meet my favourite creature of Greek mythology.

I've been very interested in the Greek myths for many years. In fact, I've written a number of different books retelling them, including several picture books.

My hope is that *Olympic Challenge!* will help spark your interest in Greek mythology. Though these stories were first told over three thousand years ago, they are still some of the most vibrant, exciting tales we have today. When we read them, it's as if we're listening to the ancient Greek storytellers across the centuries. Now that's *real* time travel, don't you think?

All my best,

Mary Pope Osborne

Prologue

One summer day in Frog Valley, a mysterious tree house appeared in the woods.

Eight-year-old Jack and his seven-year-old sister, Annie, climbed into the tree house. They found it was filled with books.

Jack and Annie soon discovered that the tree house was magic. It could take them to the places in the books. All they had to do was point to a picture and wish to be there.

Along the way, they discovered that the tree house belonged to Morgan le Fay. Morgan is a magical librarian from the time of King Arthur. She travels through time and space, gathering books.

In the Magic Tree House Books 9–12, Jack and Annie solved four ancient riddles and became Master Librarians. To help them in their *future* tasks, Morgan gave Jack and Annie secret library cards with the letters ML on them.

Jack and Annie's first four missions are to save stories from ancient libraries. This is their fourth mission . . .

1

Just One More

"You awake?" Annie's voice came out of the dark.

"Yes," said Jack from his bed.

"Get up," said Annie. "We have to get to the tree house before sunrise."

"I'm ready," said Jack.

He threw back his covers and jumped out of bed. He was wearing his jeans and T-shirt.

"Did you sleep in your clothes?" asked Annie.

"I didn't want to waste any time," said

Jack. He pulled on his rucksack.

Annie laughed. "You must really be excited about going to ancient Greece," she said.

"Yes," said Jack.

"Have you got your secret library card?" asked Annie.

"Yes, have you?" said Jack.

"Yes. Put it in your rucksack," she said. She handed her card to him. "I'll carry the torch."

"All set," said Jack.

They tiptoed downstairs and out of the door.

Outside the air was fresh and cool.

"There's no moon," said Annie. "Just stars."

She turned on her torch. "Ta-da!" she said. "Let's go."

They followed the beam of light across

their garden and up the street.

Jack was thrilled to be going to ancient Greece. But something worried him.

"What do you think will happen after we go to Greece?" he asked Annie. "Is this our last mission ever?"

"Oh, I hope not," said Annie. "What do you think?"

"I don't know. Let's ask Morgan," said Jack.

"Hurry!" Annie said.

They started running. The torch beam flew in

front of them, lighting the way.

They slowed to a walk when they got to the Frog Valley woods. The thick woods were pitch black.

Annie shone the torch upwards as they walked between the trees. Finally they found the magic tree house.

"We're here!" Annie called.

"Go on up," said Jack.

Annie grabbed the rope ladder and started up. Jack followed.

Annie shone the torch around the tree house.

Morgan le Fay was sitting at the window. She covered her eyes when the light hit her face.

"Turn off the light, please, Annie," she said softly.

Annie turned it off.

"Welcome," Morgan said in the dark.

"Are you ready for your next mission?"

"Yes!" said Annie. Then her voice got quiet. "This isn't our last one ever, is it?"

"Ask me that question after this mission," said Morgan.

"We want to go on more," said Jack.

"You're very brave to say that," said Morgan. "You've had three very hard journeys as Master Librarians."

"Oh, they weren't too hard," said Jack.

"You risked your life to save the lost story of Hercules," said Morgan.

"It was nothing," said Annie.

"*And* the Chinese story of the silk weaver," said Morgan. "And the Irish story of the serpent monster Sarph. Thank you."

"You're welcome," said Jack and Annie.

"Now," said Morgan, "for the last story . . ."

Jack heard a rustling sound.

"Here is the title," Morgan said. "You can shine your light on it, Annie."

Annie turned the torch back on. She shone it on the paper.

ΠІΥΑΣΟΣ

"Wow, is that Greek?" asked Jack.

"It certainly is," said Morgan.

She reached into her robe again and pulled out a book.

"For your research," she said.

Jack took the book from her. Annie shone her torch on the cover. They read the title: *A Day in Ancient Greece*.

"Now, what must you always

remember?" asked Morgan.

"Our research book will guide us," said Jack.

"But in our darkest hour, only the lost story can save us," said Annie.

Morgan nodded. "And you must show your secret library cards to the wisest person you meet," she said.

"Don't worry. We will. Bye!" said Annie.

Jack shivered with excitement as he pointed at the book's cover. "I wish we could go there," he said.

"And I wish we could go on lots of other missions!" Annie added.

The wind began to blow.

The tree house started to spin.

It spun faster and faster

Then everything was silent.

Absolutely silent.

2

Any Girls Here?

Jack opened his eyes. Warm sunshine streamed into the tree house.

"We definitely don't need the torch here," he said.

"Look, Morgan gave us clothes like the ones we wore in Pompeii," said Annie.

Jack looked down.

His clothes *were* similar to the ones he'd worn in the Roman town of Pompeii: a tunic and sandals. He also had a leather bag in place of his rucksack again.

Annie looked out of the window. "And

8

we landed in an olive tree – just like Pompeii!" she said.

Jack looked out of the window too. He caught his breath. "Are we in the wrong place?" he asked.

"I don't know," said Annie. "Look past the trees. Doesn't it look like a big fair?"

Jack looked. Annie was right. Past the olive grove was a field filled with white tents. Beyond the field were red-brick buildings with columns and large crowds of people.

"What's going on?" Jack asked.

He pulled the research book out of his leather bag. He found a picture of the scene outside. Below the picture were these words:

The Olympic Games began in ancient Greece over 2,500 years ago. Every four

*years, more than 40,000 people
travelled to Olympia, the town where the
festival of athletic games took place.*

"Oh, wow," Jack whispered. "We're at
the ancient Olympics!"

"Cool," said Annie.

Jack wrote in his notebook:

Olympia -
first Olympics take place

"Come on, let's go and watch!" Annie said. She started down the rope ladder.

Jack threw the notebook and the research book into his leather bag.

11

"Don't forget we have to get Morgan's story too," he said as he followed Annie.

Annie waited as Jack climbed down to the ground. Then they walked through the olive grove to where the tents were.

Jack heard pipe music and smelled food roasting over fires. Groups of men talked excitedly to one another.

"That's funny," said Annie. "I don't see any girls here."

"There *are* girls," said Jack.

"Where?" said Annie. "Show me."

Jack looked around. But he only saw men and boys – no women or girls at all.

Then he saw an outdoor theatre. A woman was standing on the stage. She had yellow hair and a purple tunic.

"There," said Jack, pointing.

"What's she doing?" asked Annie.

A soldier was on stage with her.

He wore a long cape. A helmet with a red crest hid his face.

The woman and the soldier were waving their arms and talking loudly to each other.

"I think they're doing a play," said Jack. "I'll look."

He pulled out the Greek book and found a picture of the theatre.

"Listen," he said. He read aloud:

"The Greeks were the first to write plays. Many English words to do with theatre come from Greek words, such as drama, scenery *and* chorus. *Many Greek plays are still performed today."*

"Hey, Jack," said Annie. "You're wrong."

When Jack looked up, he saw the

woman had pulled off her wig. It was a boy dressed up as a woman!

"See, even *she's* a boy," said Annie. "That's weird."

"Hmm," said Jack. He went on reading:

"A few actors would play many different parts in the same play. Women were not allowed to act, so men played the female roles too."

"That's not fair," said Annie. "What if a woman *wanted* to be in a play?"

"Don't worry about it," said Jack. He put the book away. "Let's just take a look at the Olympics, then find our story."

He nudged Annie to move along.

Just then he heard a voice.

"Wait!"

They turned round. A man with a
short white beard was walking towards
them.

"Hello," said the man. He was looking
straight at Annie. "Who are you?"

"Who are *you*?" Annie asked boldly.

3

The Secret Poet

The bearded man smiled at Annie. "My name is Plato," he said.

"Plato?" said Jack. That name sounded familiar.

"You may have heard of me," the man said. "I am a philosopher."

"What's that mean?" said Annie.

"A lover of wisdom," said Plato.

"Wow," Annie said.

Plato smiled at her. "It's odd to see a girl walking so bravely through Olympia," he said. "You must be from far

away."

"We're Jack and Annie," said Annie.
"And we come from Frog Valley. It's *very*
far away."

Plato looked puzzled.

Annie turned to Jack. "I think we
should show him our cards," she said in a
low voice. "He's a lover of wisdom."

Jack nodded. He reached into his bag
and took out the secret library cards. He
showed them to Plato.

The letters M and L that stood for
Master Librarian glittered on the cards.

"Amazing!" said Plato. "I've never met
such young Master Librarians. Why have
you come to Olympia?"

Jack pulled out the piece of paper with
the title of the story on it.

"We're looking for this story," he said.

"Oh, yes," said Plato softly. "This was

written by a brilliant poet – a friend of mine, in fact."

"Do you know where the poet lives?" asked Jack.

"Very near here," said Plato.

"Will you take us there?" asked Annie.

"Yes, but I must warn you – never tell anyone who the poet is," Plato said. "It's a secret."

"We won't," whispered Annie.

Plato led them away from the outdoor theatre.

They started down a dirt track. It was crowded with people heading for the games.

Plato stopped at the door of a sand-coloured house with a tiled roof.

He opened the door and led Jack and Annie into an empty courtyard. "Wait here," he said. He disappeared through a doorway.

Jack and Annie looked around.

Rooms opened onto the sunny courtyard. Everything was quiet.

"The people who live here must have gone to the games," said Annie.

"I bet you're right," said Jack.

He pulled out the Greek book and found a picture of a house. He read aloud:

"Men and women lived in separate parts of a Greek house. Women spent most of their time spinning and weaving and taking care of the kitchen. Boys were sent away to school when they were seven. Girls were not allowed to go to school."

"Girls can't go to school?" said Annie. "How do they learn to read and write?"

At that moment Plato returned. With him was a young woman dressed in a long tunic with a coloured border. She was holding a scroll.

Annie smiled a big smile. "*Finally*," she said. "Another girl."

"Jack and Annie, meet our secret poet," said Plato.

4

Not Fair!

The young woman smiled at Jack and
Annie.

"How did you learn to read and
write?" Annie asked.

"I taught myself," the woman
answered.

"She wrote a poem and brought it to
me," said Plato, "because I have written
and told people that I think Greek girls
should go to school and learn things."

"Is that the poem?" said Jack. He
pointed to the poet's scroll.

"Yes," said the young woman.

"It's a wonderful story," said Plato. "But she will get in trouble if it is read in our land. You must take it back to your faraway home, where it will be safe."

The poet handed Jack her scroll. He put it into his leather bag.

"Tell us your name," said Annie. "So we can tell people who wrote the story."

The young woman shook her head. "I cannot," she said. When she saw Annie's sad face, she added, "You can tell people it was written by *Anonymous*."

"*That's* your name?" asked Annie.

"No, *anonymous* means that no one knows who wrote it," said Plato.

"But that's not true!" said Annie.

"I'm afraid the risk is too great," said Plato.

Annie looked back at the woman. "I'm sorry," she said. "It's not fair – not at all."

The poet smiled at her. "I am happy

that you will take my story to your country," she said. "Perhaps some day women everywhere will write books just like men."

"They will," said Jack. "I promise."

The young woman looked at him, puzzled.

"It's true!" said Annie.

"Thank you, Annie," the young woman said. "And thank you, Jack." She bowed, then hurried out of the courtyard.

"Wait!" said Annie.

She started to go after the poet, but Plato stopped her.

"Come along," he said. "The games will start soon."

Plato then led Jack and Annie out of the Greek house back onto the dirt track.

"Girls can't write stories," grumbled Annie. "They can't go to school. They can't be in plays. I've had enough of ancient Greece. Let's get out of here."

"Wait," said Jack. "What about the Olympics?"

"Oh, yes," Annie said. Her eyes got brighter. "I almost forgot."

"Well," said Plato slowly. "I would like to take you both to the games. I have special seats in the viewing box. However . . ." He looked at Annie.

"Don't tell me," she said. "Girls can't go to the Olympics either."

Plato shook his head. "A girl will get in terrible trouble if she goes to the games," he said.

Annie sighed. "It's really, *really* not fair," she said.

"I'm sorry," said Plato. "My country is a democracy. We believe in freedom for our citizens. But I'm afraid right now that only means men."

"Annie's right. It's not fair," said Jack. "I think we should go home now."

"No, Jack. *You* go to the Olympics," said Annie. "At least you can *tell* me about it. Take notes."

"What about you?" Jack said.

"I'll go back to that play at the outdoor theatre," Annie said. "Meet me there when you're done."

Jack didn't want to leave Annie alone. But he also didn't want to miss the Olympics.

"Go! Have fun!" Annie said. She began walking away. "I'll see you later! Bye, Plato!"

"Bye, Annie," said Plato.

Annie turned back again and waved.

"I'll tell you all about it!" Jack called.

"This way," said Plato.

He and Jack turned and joined the
crowd heading towards the Olympic
grounds.

5

Hi, Zeus

"This is the very first day of the games," Plato told Jack, "the day of the chariot races."

"Oh, wow," whispered Jack.

He couldn't believe he was going to see a chariot race. The modern Olympic Games didn't have chariot races.

They walked towards the race track. Plato pointed to a large building near the road.

"That is the gymnasium," he said. "It is where our athletes train. They practise running and throwing the javelin and discus."

"We have a gymnasium at our school in Frog Valley," said Jack. "We call it a gym."

"People all over the world copy us Greeks," Plato said.

"Wait," said Jack. "I have to take notes for Annie."

He pulled out his notebook and wrote:

Ancient Greeks invented gyms

"OK, we can go," said Jack. He tucked his notebook under his arm.

As they moved along, Plato pointed to a beautiful tree nearby.

"The olive tree is our sacred tree," he said. "The winners of the games will wear crowns made from its branches."

"Oh, wow," said Jack. And he wrote:

Olive tree is sacred

Next they passed a beautiful statue of a winged lady.

"Who's that?" said Jack.

"She's Nike, the goddess of victory," said Plato.

Jack quickly wrote:

Nike is goddess of victory

"Nike is important to the games," said Plato. "But the most important Olympic god is in there."

He took Jack to a brick building with huge columns. They stepped through the door. It was a temple. Jack gasped.

In front of them loomed the biggest

statue he had ever seen.

The statue was at least two storeys high. It was of a bearded man sitting on a throne.

"This is the temple of Zeus. And that is a statue of Zeus himself," said Plato.

"The Olympic Games are played in his honour. He is the chief god of the Greek gods and goddesses."

"Oh, wow," whispered Jack.

"Yesterday all the athletes came here," said Plato. "They swore to Zeus that they had trained for ten months. And they promised to obey the rules of the games."

The statue of the mighty Greek god stared down at Jack.

Jack felt very small. "Hi, Zeus," he said. His voice was small too.

Suddenly, trumpet sounds came from outside.

"The hour has come," said Plato. "We must hurry. The Olympic parade begins!"

6

Mystery Man

Plato and Jack hurried past the crowds standing at the sides of the race track. Everyone was shouting and cheering.

"I have seats next to the judges," said Plato. He pointed to a tall stand with rows of benches.

Plato led Jack through the crowd and up the steps to their seats.

"Wow, thanks," said Jack.

He had a great view.

The Olympic parade had already started. Musicians playing pipes were

at the front. Behind them marched the
Olympic athletes – the best in all of
Greece.

Jack sighed as he watched the parade
going around the track. *Annie would
really love this*, he thought.

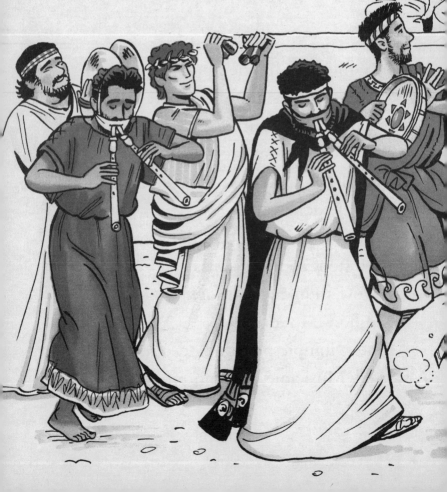

"The athletes in front
are the runners," said
Plato. "Foot races are
the oldest event of the
Olympics."

Jack pulled out his
notebook and wrote:

Oldest event is foot races

"Behind the runners are the boxers," said Plato. "They're wearing special gloves and bronze helmets."

Jack wrote:

Boxers wear gloves and helmets

"Behind them are the wrestlers," said Plato.

And Jack wrote:

Wrestlers

When he looked up again, he saw
a soldier staring up at him from the
sidelines.

The soldier was dressed like the actor

from the outdoor
theatre. He had on
a long cape and a
red crested helmet
that covered most
of his face.

But something
was strange. This soldier
was short – *really* short.

"Here come the discus
and javelin throwers,"
said Plato, "and then the
men in armour."

"What do they do?"
asked Jack.

"They race wearing
full armour," said Plato.

Jack smiled to
himself. He knew
Annie would think that

was funny.

He wrote in his notebook:

Some runners race in armour

Jack finished writing.

He looked back at the short soldier.

"In a moment, the chariot races will begin," said Plato. "Winning a chariot race is the greatest honour of the games."

Jack just nodded. He was still studying the short soldier, who seemed to be looking back at him.

Suddenly a small hand came out from the soldier's cape. The hand gave a little wave.

Jack gasped. It was Annie's hand waving!

The short soldier was *Annie*.

7

Go! Go! Go!

Jack stared in horror at Annie. She must have borrowed a costume from the theatre!

He remembered Plato's words: *A girl will get in terrible trouble if she tries to attend the Olympic Games.*

Jack shook his head at her and pointed his finger, as if to say, *Get out of here!*

But Annie just waved at him again.

Jack kept shaking his head at Annie. He even shook his fist.

Annie turned back to watch the race.

"It's not a joke!" Jack shouted.

Plato turned and looked at him. "Of course not," he said. "We take the games very seriously."

Jack felt his face grow hot. He glared at Annie's back.

Just then the trumpet sounded.

"The chariots are taking their places," said Plato.

Jack saw the dozens of chariots lined up on the race track. Each chariot was pulled by four horses.

Jack glanced back at Annie. She was looking up at him, pointing at the chariots.

The trumpet sounded again.

The horses set off!

The crowd went wild. They were cheering and screaming and stamping their feet.

Clouds of dust rose up as the chariots
raced around the track.

Annie turned back to watch the race.
She began jumping up and down.

"Go! Go! Go!" she shouted.

A few people began staring at the strange small soldier with the high-pitched voice.

Jack couldn't take it any more. He had to get Annie away before it was too late! He shoved his notebook into his bag. "I have to go!" he shouted to Plato.

The philosopher looked surprised. Jack was afraid to tell him that Annie had broken the rules.

"I had a great time. But I have to go home now," he said. "Thanks for everything!"

"Have a safe journey," said Plato.

Jack waved and started down the steps. As he climbed down, he saw Annie pull off her helmet.

Her ponytail flew up and down as she jumped and shouted, "Go! Go! Go!"

Her soldier's cape fell off.

Now *lots* of people were staring at her. Someone shouted for the guards.

Annie was too busy cheering to notice anything.

Jack moved as quickly as he could.

But two big guards got to Annie first.

8

Save Annie!

The guards tried to pull Annie away
from the chariot race.

Annie looked surprised. Then she
looked angry. "Let go of me!" she
shouted.

Jack rushed down the steps of the
viewing stand.

The guards were having a hard time
pulling Annie through all the people.

"Leave her alone!" Jack yelled.

His voice was lost in the noise of the
race.

He pushed his way through the crowd. "Leave her alone!" he kept shouting. "Leave her alone!"

Finally Jack reached Annie and the guards. He tried to grab her, but a guard blocked his way.

"Let her go!" yelled Jack. "I promise I'll take her home!"

More guards arrived. The crowd began to shout, "Arrest her! Arrest her!"

The guards kept pulling Annie away.

"Jack! The story!" cried Annie.

Of course! thought Jack. *The poet's story! This is definitely our darkest hour!*

He reached into his bag and pulled out the poet's scroll.

He held the story up to the sky. "Save Annie!" he shouted.

But Jack's voice was again lost in the roar of the race as the four-horse chariots barrelled through the dust.

Jack looked around wildly for someone – or something – to help them.

Then suddenly the crowd fell silent.

All heads turned to watch as a huge white horse galloped out of the dust.

The crowd murmured with excitement and wonder.

The white horse was the most
beautiful animal Jack had ever seen.
He was pulling an empty chariot.
And he was galloping straight towards Jack.

9

Fly Away Home

The white horse stopped at the low wall
by the edge of the track.

"He's come for *us*!" cried Annie.

The guards stared in awe at the horse.

Annie broke free and dashed over to
Jack. He grabbed her hand and they ran
to the horse.

The guards shouted and started after
them.

But they were too late. Jack and Annie
had already climbed over the wall and
into the waiting chariot.

"Go! Go! Go!" Annie cried to the huge white horse.

The horse reared and pawed the air.

The crowd stepped back from the wall.

The guards froze.

Jack looked up to where Plato was now standing. Plato smiled and waved at him.

Then the white horse leaped forward, pulling the chariot behind him.

Jack couldn't even wave back at Plato. All he could do was hold on tight as the horse galloped beside the Olympic racers.

Jack bounced up and down. Dust and sand got in his eyes. He squeezed them shut and crouched down in the chariot.

He didn't know where they were going. But it didn't matter. The white horse was in charge.

Jack heard the thundering noise of the racing horses and chariots. He heard the screaming crowd.

He felt sand blowing in his face and the hard bumping and rattling of the chariot.

Suddenly he was thrown backwards. He heard a *swoosh* of wind, then . . .

Silence.

"Oh, wow!" cried Annie.

Jack opened his eyes. All he saw was blue sky. He pushed his glasses into place and looked around.

"Help!" he cried.

The white horse had grown giant feathery wings and was pulling their chariot into the sky.

Jack gripped the railing of the chariot and held on for dear life.

"To the tree house!" shouted Annie.

Below, the Olympic crowd watched in stunned silence.

The winged
horse left the games
behind and flew
over the temple of Zeus,
over the statue of Nike, over the
sacred olive tree and the gymnasium.

On they went: over the poet's house,
the Greek theatre, and the field of white
tents.

Finally the winged horse coasted to
the ground near the olive grove.

The wheels of the chariot bumped
onto the grass. Then slowly, slowly, they
came to a stop.

Jack and Annie stepped out of the

chariot. Jack's legs were so wobbly he
could hardly walk.

Annie rushed to the horse and stroked
his neck.

"Thank you," she whispered.

Jack patted the horse's long white neck
too. "Thanks," he said. "That was the best
ride of my life."

The horse snorted and pawed the ground.

"Come on, Annie. We have to go before they find us," said Jack.

"I don't want to leave him," said Annie. "He's the most beautiful horse in the whole world." Her eyes filled with tears.

"We have to," said Jack.

The horse put his head down and touched Annie's forehead with his soft nose. Then he gave her a gentle push towards the tree house.

Annie sniffled but started walking. Jack took her hand as they walked through the olive grove to the rope ladder of the tree house.

"You first," Jack said.

Annie started up the ladder. Jack followed.

When they were inside, Annie hurried

to the window. Jack grabbed the Frog Valley book.

He pointed to a picture of the woods and said, "I wish—"

"Look!" said Annie.

Jack looked out of the window. The horse had spread his great feathery wings. He was rising from the field.

The white horse flew high into the blue Olympian sky.

Then he disappeared behind the clouds.

"Bye!" called Annie. A tear rolled down her cheek.

Jack pointed again at the Frog Valley book. "I wish we could go there," he said.

The wind started to blow.

The tree house began to spin.

It spun faster and faster.

Then everything was still.

Absolutely still.

10

They're All Here

Jack opened his eyes.

It was so dark he couldn't see anything.

He felt his clothes. He was wearing his T-shirt and jeans again. The leather bag had turned back into his rucksack.

"Hello," said Morgan le Fay. Her voice came from the corner of the tree house.

"Hi!" said Annie.

"Did you have a good journey?" asked Morgan.

"I did," said Jack, "but girls can't do

anything fun in ancient Greece."

"I did *one* fun thing," Annie said wistfully. "I rode in a chariot pulled by a flying horse."

"That must have been wonderful," said Morgan. "You were very lucky to be bringing me the story of Pegasus."

"Who?" said Jack.

"Pegasus," said Morgan. "He's the great white winged horse in Greek mythology."

"Oh, yes," said Jack. "I think I've heard of him."

He felt in his rucksack and found the scroll. He gave it to Morgan. He could still barely see her in the dark.

"It was written by Anonymous," said Annie.

"I know," said Morgan. "Many talented women used that name in the

past. Her story will be a great addition to my Camelot library."

"Plato helped us find it," said Jack.

"Ah, my good friend Plato," said Morgan. "He was one of the greatest thinkers who ever lived."

"And Pegasus was the greatest horse,"

60

said Annie. She sighed. "I just wish I could see him again."

"You can," Morgan said softly. "He's here right now."

"Pegasus?" cried Annie. "Oh wow!"

Annie turned on the torch and used it to find her way down the rope ladder.

Jack grabbed his rucksack and followed her.

When they were both standing on the ground, Annie shone her torch at the dark trees.

"Pegasus?" she said. "Where are you? Pegasus?"

"Turn off your torch, Annie," said Morgan. She was looking down from the tree-house window.

Annie switched off the light.

"In the night, you can see *all* the story characters that saved you on your last four missions," said Morgan. "They are all here – Hercules and the silk weaver, Sarph, the serpent monster, and Pegasus."

Jack pushed his glasses into place and studied the dark woods.

"Where are they, Morgan?" cried Annie. "Where's Pegasus?"

"Look hard," said Morgan.

"I can't see him!" said Annie.

"Yes, you can," said Morgan. "The old stories are always with us. We are never alone."

Has Morgan gone crazy? wondered Jack.

"Look up," said Morgan. "Your friends are in the night sky. They are stars."

"Stars?" whispered Jack.

He stared at the shimmering field of tiny stars overhead.

"Hercules is a constellation," said Morgan. "The Romans imagined him

62

kneeling in the sky, holding a club over his head."

Morgan waved her finger at the sky. For a moment Jack saw a living, breathing Hercules outlined by stars.

"And there's the silk weaver, with her beloved cowherd," said Morgan. "The ancient Chinese believed that they were two stars on either side of the Milky Way."

She waved her hand again. The lovely silk weaver was outlined in the heavens.

"And long ago, the Irish believed the Milky Way itself was the serpent monster Sarph," said Morgan.

She waved her hand. A giant serpent glittered through the sky.

"And the ancient Greeks named one of their constellations Pegasus," said Morgan.

She waved her hand again and the

white horse's head, wings and galloping legs glowed in the sky.

"I see him!" said Annie. Then she whispered, "I love you, Pegasus."

Jack thought he saw the stars move as if Pegasus was rearing back in the sky.

After a breathless moment of silence, Morgan lowered her arm. The night sky became a field of tiny glittering stars again.

"You have done amazing work as Master Librarians," she said. "I would trust you with any important mission."

"Does that mean we're going on more trips?" asked Jack.

"Indeed it does," said Morgan. "*Many* more."

Jack smiled with relief.

"When is our next mission?" asked Annie.

"As soon as I need your help, I will send for you," said Morgan. "Go home now and rest."

"Goodbye," said Annie.

"Goodbye," said Jack.

"Farewell," said Morgan.

There was a sudden rushing of

wind, then a blur of blinding light. And Morgan le Fay and the magic tree house vanished.

The night was still.

"Home?" asked Annie.

"Yes," said Jack.

As they walked between the trees, the Frog Valley woods were pitch black.

Jack couldn't see a thing.

But he didn't ask Annie to turn on the torch. For once, he wasn't worried about finding his way home.

He felt as if someone – or something – was leading them through the woods.

Morgan's words came back to him: *The old stories are always with us. We are never alone.*

Jack looked up at the stars again. They were beginning to fade in the growing light of dawn.

But he thought he could hear the beating of giant wings, somewhere high above.

More Facts for You and Jack

The Olympics

The Olympics of ancient Greece were held for over a thousand years, from 776 BC to AD 384.

Every four years, the games were held in several cities, including the town of Olympia, for five days in August. (The modern Olympics were named after Olympia.)

For two months, all fighting and wars ceased so people could travel safely to and from the Olympics.

The first modern Olympics were held in Athens, Greece, in 1896.

Greek athletes believed that having a physically fit body was a way to honour their chief god, Zeus. Olympia's statue of Zeus was one of the seven wonders of the ancient world. Unfortunately, it no longer exists.

Greek Language

The word *anonymous* comes from a Greek word that means "nameless".

The English language has many words that were originally Greek, especially words to do with sports, such as *gymnasium*, *marathon* and *athlete*; words to do with science, such as *psychology* and *astronomy*; and words related to the arts, such as *drama*, *theatre* and *scenery*.

The word *museum* is also of Greek origin.
Over 2,000 years ago, the Greeks built
a temple to the nine goddesses known
as the Muses. They called the temple the
Museum.

Some Greek letters are similar to ours.
The Greek A is called *alpha*. The B is
called *beta*. That's where we get our word
alphabet.

Democracy

About 2,500 years ago, the Greeks
adopted a system of government called
a *democracy*. Under the Greek democracy,
all citizens had a say in the government.
At that time, however, women and slaves
were not considered citizens.

Plato

Plato the philosopher lived in ancient Greece in the fourth century BC. He founded a school called the Academy. In both his teachings and his writings, Plato explored the best way for a government to be set up. His ideas are still talked about today.

Zeus

Zeus was god of the skies and ruler of all the Greek gods and goddesses. Zeus and his family were called Olympians because they lived on top of a mountain called Mount Olympus. The major Greek gods and goddesses were later adopted by the Romans. Zeus was called Jupiter by the Romans.

Pegasus

In Greek mythology, a great winged horse sprang from the neck of a snake-haired monster known as Medusa. The horse was named Pegasus, which may come from a Greek word that means "spring". Pegasus was tamed by a young man named Bellerophon.

Star Myths

In ancient times, mythic characters from different world cultures were sometimes identified as patterns of stars in the night sky. Once a hero or heroine took a place in the heavens, he or she became famous for ever.